BOO, BUNNY!

Kathryn O. Galbraith

Illustrated by Jeff Mack

HARCOURT, INC.   Orlando Austin New York San Diego London   Manufactured in China

One shy bunny.
One dark night.

One hungry eye . . .
two crooked teeth . . .
one rattle of bones . . .
two scaly feet!

One soft **whooooooo!**

One loud booOOO!

Jump.

Bump!

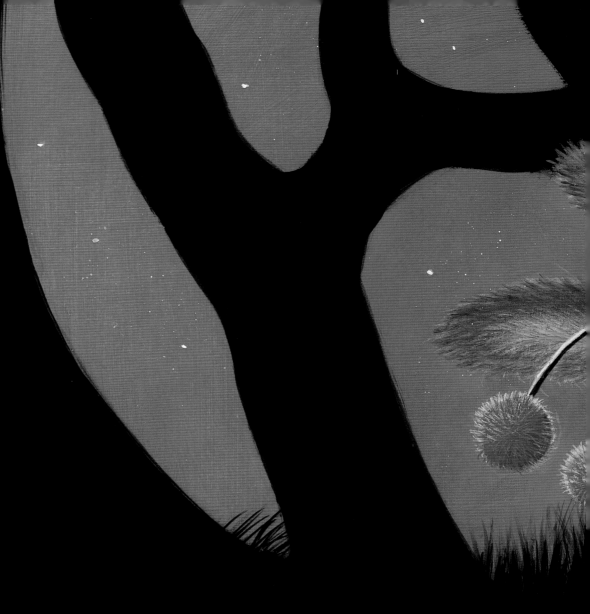

"Eeek!"

Hop-

One bunny quivers.

One bunny shivers.

One big door.
One hissing cat.

"Trick or treat,"
whispers one.

"TRICK OR TREAT!"

shout two.

creak!

The door opens wide.

Two giant hops.

One loud

Whoooooo!

Two bunnies giggle.

"whooo-booo to you!"

One silver moon.
Two paws held tight.

Two brave bunnies.
One Halloween night.

To the family on Auburn Street.
And once again to Steve.—K. O. G.

For Kellie and Dillon—J. M.

Text copyright © 2008 by Kathryn O. Galbraith
Illustrations copyright © 2008 by Jeffrey M. Mack

Library of Congress Cataloging-in-Publication Data
Galbraith, Kathryn Osebold.
Boo, bunny!/Kathryn O. Galbraith; [illustrated by] Jeff Mack.
p.   cm.
Summary: Two small bunnies face their fears while trick-or-treating on Halloween night.
[1. Fear—Fiction.   2. Rabbits—Fiction.   3. Halloween—Fiction.   4. Stories in rhyme.]
I. Mack, Jeff, ill.   II. Title.
PZ8.3.G1216Boo   2008
[E]—dc22   2007021426
ISBN 978-0-15-216246-7

First edition
H G F E D C B A

The illustrations in this book were done in acrylic on watercolor paper.
The display type was set in House of Terror and Spookhouse.
The text type was set in Chaloops and Spookhouse.
Color separations by Chroma Graphics (Overseas) Pte. Ltd., Singapore
Manufactured by South China Printing Company, Ltd., China
Production supervision by Pascha Gerlinger
Designed by Michele Wetherbee